THE VERY IMPATIENT CATERPILLAR

Ross Burach

Scholastic Inc.

WAIT?!

You're telling me I can become a BUTTERFLY?

With wings?

For REAL?

Yes.

Yes.

Yes.

Wait for ME!!

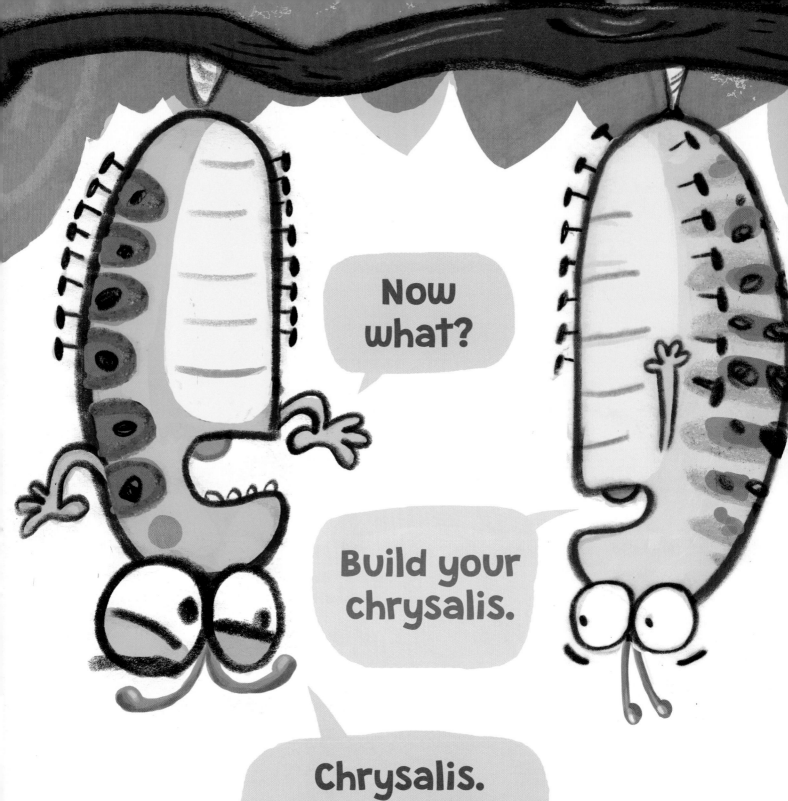

8

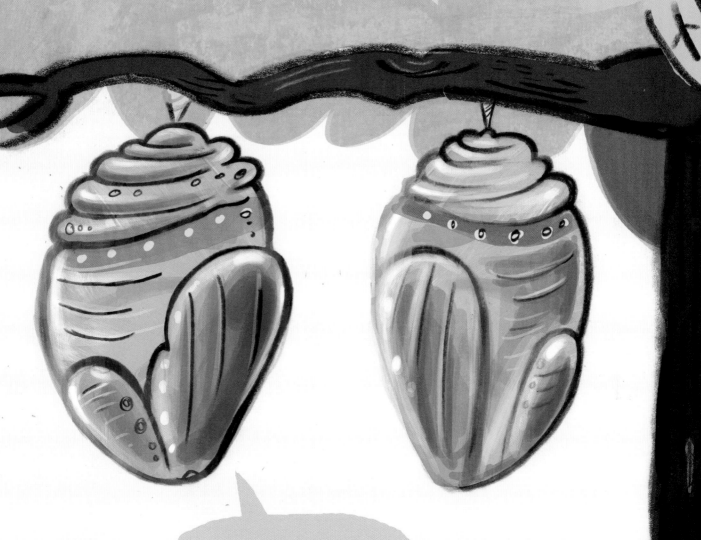

HHH!
TO METAMORPHOSIZE!

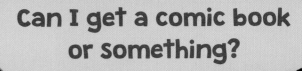

Look out world.
Feast your eyes on this beautiful . . .

WAIT!!!

Where are my wings?

Time for a new approach.

22

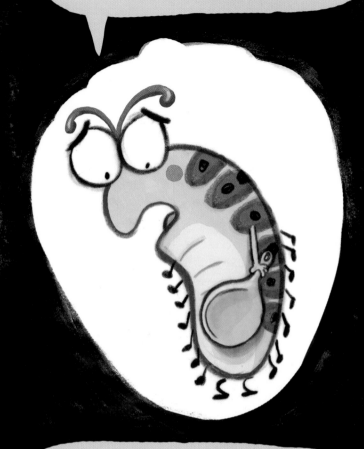

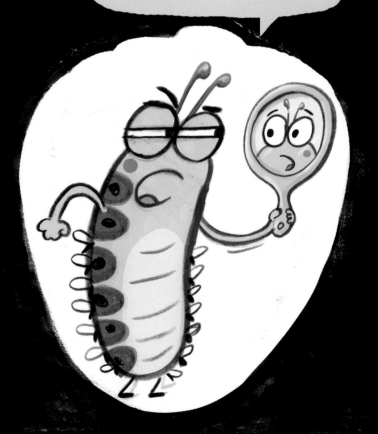

Day 1

Day 2

Day 3

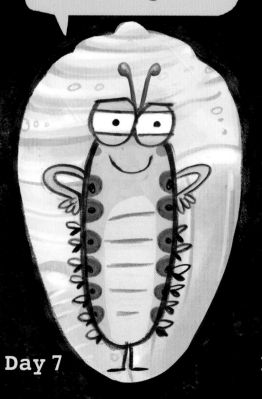

Day 7

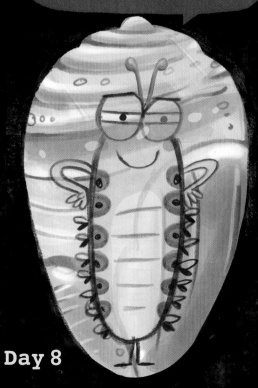

Day 8

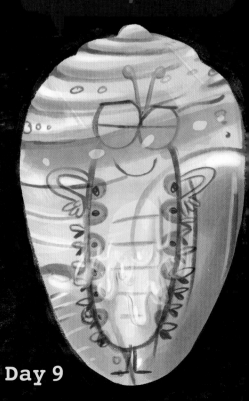

Day 9

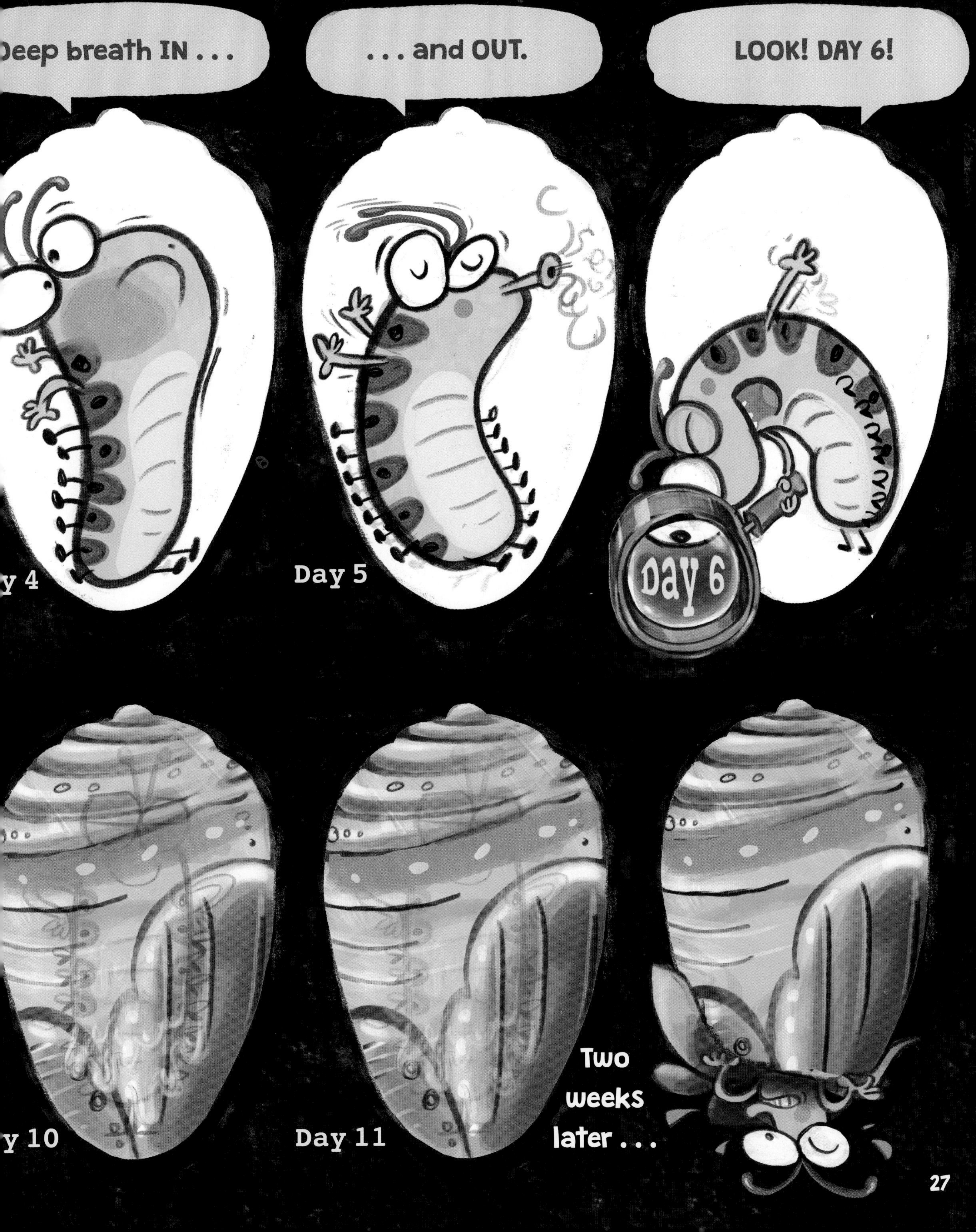

Deep breath IN . . .
. . . and OUT.
LOOK! DAY 6!
y 4
Day 5
DAY 6
y 10
Day 11
Two
weeks
later . . .

I did it! I'm a

BUTTERFLY!

HEY! Where are you all going?

We're migrating.

Migrating. Right. Right. **WAIT FOR ME!**

For Mom, thank you
for always being so patient.

Ross Burach's art was created with pencil, crayon, acrylic paint, and digital coloring. · The text type was set in Grandstander Classic Bold. · The display type was set in Grandstander Classic Bold.
Production was overseen by Angie Chen. · Manufacturing was supervised by Shannon Rice.
The book was art directed by Marijka Kostiw, designed by Ross Burach and Marijka Kostiw, and edited by Tracy Mack.

Scholastic Inc., 557 Broadway, New York, NY 10012